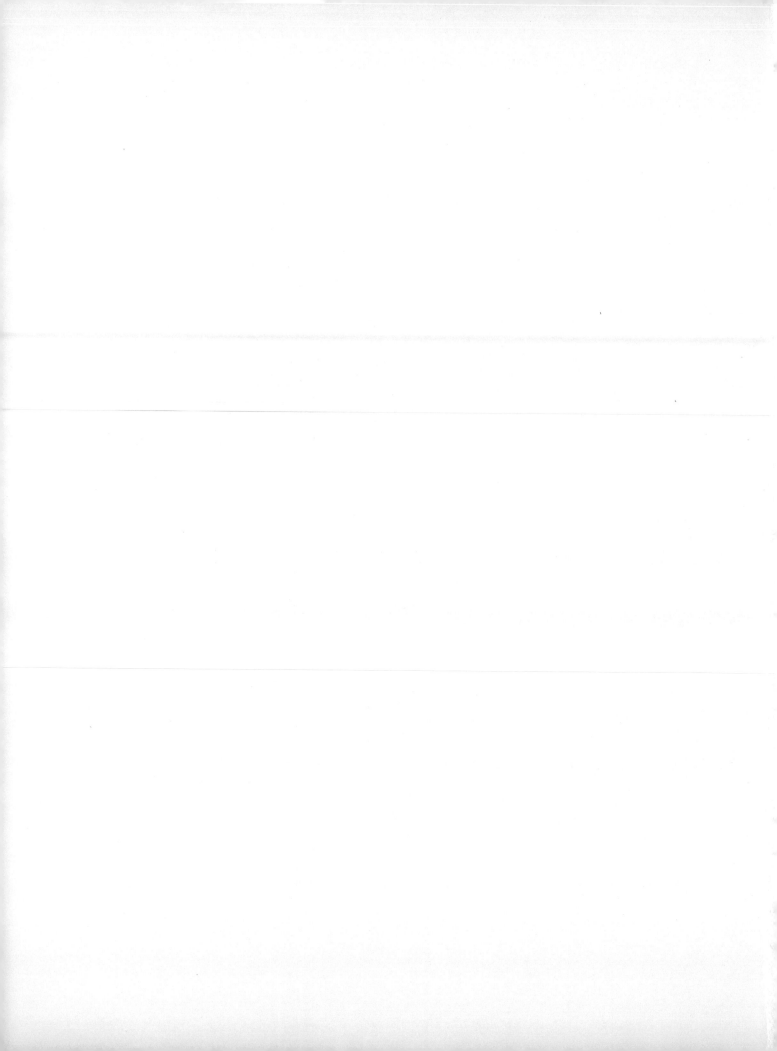

World So Wide

from *New York Times*
bestselling author
Alison McGhee

with illustrations by
Kate Alizadeh

two lions

Published by Two Lions, New York • www.apub.com
Amazon, the Amazon logo, and Two Lions are trademarks of Amazon.com, Inc., or its affiliates.
ISBN-13: 9781542006330 • ISBN-10: 1542006333

The illustrations were created digitally.
Book design by Abby Dening
Printed in China • First Edition
10 9 8 7 6 5 4 3 2 1

To Jillian Pang, with so much love –A.M.

To Hilary –K.A.

Somewhere in the world,
the world so far,
the world so wide,

someone is the
youngest person alive.

Picture them
just opening their eyes.

What will be the
first sights they *see*?

Sun and moon and sky . . .

the love in someone's eye?

What will be the
first sounds they **hear**?

Wind and rain and birds . . .
someone whispering gentle words?

What will be the
first things they **smell**?

Flowers and trees and summer breeze . . .
a funny puppy's fur?

What will be the
first things they **touch**?

Blanket and bunny,
toes and tummy . . .

the arms of
someone warm?

Did you know that long ago,
at the moment they were born,

everyone in this world so wide
was once the youngest person alive?

Even me?

Even you.

You looked at us
with wide, deep eyes,
and we smiled back at you.

So much you wanted to say,
so much we wanted to hear,
so many firsts along the way. . . .

And maybe on some far-off day,
if you're as lucky as me,
the newest person in the world
will open their eyes to see
a grown-up you smiling back at them.

Through the days and through the nights,
you'll hold that baby tight
and love them with all your might.

You'll show them a life
that's bright and true,
so ever after,

when they think of you,
the world will feel

full of love . . .

and soft
and sweet
and new.